A POETRY BOOK

DREAM STATION

ADELEINE KEANE

For September

*And I witness your beauty fade to grey; eyes
barely alive as once were. When the breaking point
comes to scold my infantile stargazing, my
delirium urges me forward through time, tears
pouring from shackled, bruised mind. Hands cling
upon cold skin, breaking loose memories unkind.*

*'Tis but a chance to dream, washing away ill-
wrenched thought.*

A POETRY BOOK

DREAM STATION

palemode

DREAM STATION
from palemode

Copyright © 2021 Palemode, LLC
All rights reserved. No part of this book may be reproduced in any form or by any electronic or mechanical means, including information storage and retrieval systems, without written permission from the author, except for the use of brief quotations in a book review.

This book is a work of fiction. Names, characters, businesses, places, events and incidents are either the products of the author's imagination or used in a fictitious manner. Any resemblance to actual persons, living or dead, or actual events is purely coincidental.

Author Info: **www.adeleinekeane.com**
Editor: Adeleine Keane

For rights & permissions or additional queries, please visit www.palemode.com

First Edition: March 2021
Revised March 2024
10 9 8 7 6 5 4 3 2 1

pISBN: 979-8-9903662-1-3

CONTENTS

BEHIND MACHIAVELLIAN EYES

PORTRAITURES OF PERFECTION

*If by uninhabited gaze, you come by education,
and blank tongue become your sole collation. With
weeping lips, stretched by indecent force. Illicit rev-
elation by way of finely threaded cloth — coarse.
To retain whilst soaked with cherry-crimson inoc-
ulation, scarring virgin mind, whereby they push
to endorse dilation.*

CHIMERA

I peel back my image of a child;
'tis not my intention to be mild.
Not one who plays that beautiful flute;
for juvenile ears are deaf, and I am but mute.

And we are not enchanters of credulous mind;
merely wordsmiths, tempering words defined.
To use upon, not chimera who dance — instead
the lost, who love to read and be read.

W. FRED

Look upon ole, frolicking Fred,
Skipping stones by the watershed
Where he finds joy in his chosen fad;
Not soured by fears of being slightly mad

Where he bends down by birch tree,
While other folks would, but flee;
To pull iron crow with childish glee
And with high hopes and plenty pursuit —

Whacks once, twice, and three,
Then takes keen work to knee
To rustle up his world-famous gum,
Nice and thick — wouldn't you agree?

And you could cook up your own gum;
Nice and thick — and free

PRIME EMULSION

What are simplistic forms, but
possessing all the grounds for reason:
To recycle cognition into skill and direction;
point mast and sail towards graduated season,
playing deity with a single drip of emulsion;
shape simple-minded cells into propulsion.

With single erection, spring virgin construct;
and from the sludge of complex division,
omnipotent shepherds must erect revision.
Far-reaching procedure, unseen men provision,
with severed sensory concepts way of incision.

PIOUS & PERSPICACITY

Reason me not to treason — leave me;
lest I know whom I am judged, set free.
To care is cumbersome, worse, and weak;
behind eyes of indoctrinated, ready to shriek.

Listen child: For deaf ear and large beak;
can shout louder and dare not speak.
Waddle with babbling, warped tongue;
poked not, prodded not; only riches sung.

Read my small life fare, decisive and just;
'tis, not you who breaks rules — you must.
Within this rotten tomb of empty knowledge;
grows fear revered, in insufferable college.

Look beyond the agile, pious fool;
engrossed in their splendid betting pool.
Not minding the trajectory of shriveled pages —
'tis not within them to read advice from sages.

AGNEAU VERTUEUX

Break coffer and crown, over the theological imp:
For it makes commandments, like a duplicitous
   simp.
With rose, delinquent podium, it concocts a plan:
To rule rigidly over what guides child into man.

It conjures very little attempt, at most things;
except on special days — grows baron fangs.
With Aristotle eye, penetrates self-reliance,
and implants grim fears — seeds victimized
   alliance.

Cast aside adorned trappings to purify forlorn
   boys;
playing judge and jury to unsuspecting prac-
   titioner,
unbeknownst of righteous devices it spiritually
   employs.

With vampish prick and condemnation —
   prisoner
of form and aeonian temptation.

TALE OF THE STAGRAPUR

scrutinize the blind stagrapur — they drivel
with large crayon: scrabble and scribble
they morph anecdote into pablum to nibble
can't you comprehend their unending quibble

gaze upon the obtuse serpent of shallow and repute
shower them with relevance; they can not refute
yet what a travesty, for they lack the proper
*   pursuit*
to conjure knowledge from their handheld fruit

look upon the well versed and quick versifier
they whelp for nothing with titanium pacifier

alas, they know not of the teaming anxiety
that burns bright in thinkers' past, lost in utter
*   piety*
mind's defects untouched, favor juvenile im-
*   propriety*

for the stagrapur does not seek awareness
breaching only as far as the shallow epidermis
for this modern-day beast does not seek integrity
only notoriety

CHROMATIQUE

Look upon the lovely locks of Marianne.
Most Sundays skewed and distorted,
from ravaged reflections made by man —
to tell a child how she consorted.

Ivory bundles of pearl that gleam,
adorning neck in hopeful arrogance.
Unmarked tube and vials of cream;
mask abused arms, with sheer elegance.

MATTER OF DIAPAUSE

The rooms of my mind burn red ember,
as cold as your heart in late December.
When you would scream at the night,
like a banshee broken from afforded flight.

When you would calm down from your perch:
Your fear, like lineage, would trickle into church.
Where you would absolve sins and be forgotten;
though bloody hearts would remain torn and
  rotten.

On those cold days when I lay frightened — still,
I understood that you could not pull away (shrill
from cackling voices in your warped head);
gurgle and retch undigested hearts — dead.

Valkyrie of modern man and child — mind's
  ladder.
Reprieve tiny body back to synthetic surficial,
to create concoction of tears and weak bladder.

Awaken to dreams of hysteria: trembling thumb,
self-tailored glass — afterglow — my feelings
  numb,
and my fledgling brain becomes tossed and dumb.

Strange how steel, it permeates weirdly organic;
giving me pause to escape passing panic.
With head down, collapsed to newfound news;
oh, how I envy those who wriggle in their pews.

Feathers of the soul soon molt, ever slighted;
like dew that bounces from budding fruit, un-
      invited.

And though I find your darkened hair flawed.
And though I find your moody eyes odd;
it was them most of all that I can forever trace;
unendingly putting tears to my worn, etched face.

And after the matter has ended, the act you played
creates distilled illusion, forever reckoning —
      stayed.
In my foolish, feeble, and childish desire for more
leaves me vacuous, bleeding out as before.

RECAPITULATION

I ask you strained, feeble louse,
with tepid hands weighted upon blouse.

'Twas not you who scorns flesh — begin
to bear fruit, only cast aside in the end.
Though becoming ripe with splendor,
cold from barren earth: surrender.

Strip to swallow the nectar of disillusion,
where you beg and barter towards collusion.

To drive loved ones away to war: For
you take solace in walking streets — swore
you'd grasp each member of court tender;
taking heads, colliding them in a blender.

For sake of child's play — transfusion;
and render the entirety of life in confusion.

Disregard others with fitful rage, recessed;
a succubus searching for next possessed.
Although others tried many a time, broken,
to give you delicacies cooked up — bespoken.

Forsaking one's morality — stained;
with admirable intentions unexplained.
Whether watchful moment of waxy knight
or dreary, drunken stallion, you lose sight.

With adequate sung condition and lure;
trade health of your sprite — pure.

For moments tryst into the sea of sin:
Trade token glyphs of your kin;
creating illusions that taste bitter — fain;
though in the end, all that remains is pain.

How you pay yourself no mind or growth;
you, who takes no heed of your oath,
to swaddle your own so they didn't fold;
to a two-dog night that has taken hold.

Pitching tents while they slept coldly,
never to be unearthed, ever so fondly.

So I ask, you artist of your unraveling.
What do you grasp of foreboding — baffling.
While others celebrated your undoing;
I, in stasis, reeling from knowing — stewing.

A FRACTURED CROWN

As mode shifts from jaunty to passé:
The plump cherubs, nestled within hay,
Would wrench head to laugh feverishly;
Towards cracked crown fitted generously
Adorned heads, now disillusioned and bleak;
Without moral position, how dare they speak
With lords, once proud and proper to court,
Now find themselves in streets — torn apart

Outcast serpents slip into virtuous clothing;
Proper creatures morph by sheer loathing
Nature beckons them inward to disillusion;
Once the sane and ever understanding illusion
Men reside on fringes through Malthusianism;
Divinity of articulation replaced by fascism
Waxy ideals and blood pour from lost eye;
Blind forsaken — assimilated by winged fly

Expanding season cycle cross bleak night,
Leaving twinkling trails bursting in flight
Misty, morning woodlands conjure chorus;
Basking raptors assume flight for Horus
Tearful tracks dissolve under salvia;
Fearful acts in passion ignite heart of Aliyah
Fauna pauperized, not by standing philosophy,
But thrown askew by coveted, wicked curiosity

Apparitions masquerade among shade;
Bodies howl fierce and in an instant fade;
A cycle of ordinances come with a thud,
Crumbling church — painted in blood
Newly birthed babes come to ink thought;
Stitched eyes, bandaged ears — untaught
Cull Trojan flies from sprawling carob,
Stepping over smoldering cherub

FALLEN BEAST

Dost thou dwell in teaming cult of admiration,
With sheepish sharp bite and blunt intention
Derelict verse — burnt papyrus and pen of men;
Scratching at tender orifice to listen once again

Your unseen rehearse harsh memories — hi-
        bernated;
Where insignificant forms and thoughts are
        violated
Worship on ivory rostrum; stock streets, bifurcated;
Beastly, innocent bodies maltreated — assimilated

Sheep scamper to school for suppressed behavior;
Affluent orphans passed up, given societal waiver
To go out and act in ways that are unsavory,
Though evil intentions create disillusioned bravery

Plasma addles around those who conform position,
On a splintered pedestal built by conjugal
        condition
And from emotive sepsis would come intimate
        truth,
To incite innocent eyes from prefabricated proof

And if I were thy lamb, would throbbing feeling,
In the chamber of tumid potentates, pour thin
And would others come down from proceeding,
To catch my dripping fervor with their chin

With iniquitous, outreached hand and slippery
>>*tongue,*
Thou obscure to recall motley life in pleasure and
>>*pain;*
Newly birthed ideas and purpose silenced among
The hamlet of abundance and commercially same

PLURALISM

Throw thy prideful ticker-tape parade,
for bleak, ebony 'noon shimmers a tirade.
Porous Gaia peels from globular flood;
in time, Themis crumbles by corrosive blood.
Wretch, mute voices cry out in a night rotten;
dead eyes cast on a body already forgotten.

WHAT BECOMES OF DREAMS

PORTRAITURES OF IMPERMANENCE

What my child, can I profess upon you that you haven't already heard. What my child, can I illustrate to you that you haven't already glimpsed. What child can I teach you that I am first unable to learn? For in the gray corners of my fading senses, it is through your past that I must master my care for you.

NIGHT SPECTRE

I, preoccupied with distilled visions of vexation,
awaken by sounds of articulation — cause
    taxation.
Not with pulp and soma, but troubled vocalization;
milky oculus and heart-wretched mind: causation.

Illness sets, burning eyes, and hubris — sancti-
    monious.
Solution abound (hand primed); harmonious.
With heaven's ponderous expansion of translation;
you, however, chose to stare into mirror's in-
    dignation.

EMPTY CUP

Depravation permeates thy mind:
Ruptures loose memories unkind.
Tosses out the intricacies of a child,
once beguiled, now tooled — compiled.
Deliberation and tenderness replaced;
indifference and wisdom interlaced.
With eyes fixated on hereafter,
and memory thy master:
Thou reflect not,
know not,
reason not.

SOAP SOLVENT

I postulate the profound sea of unrest;
though you shall not see my contempt.
Benevolent babes rinse away the rest;
washing away ill-advised attempt.

Unresolved marks catalyze platitude —
careful child, decipher the ideals of adventurism.
Meander the credo of mandated, worn attitude;
eyes reflect truth that mind lacks latitude.

BROKEN REGRET

What is a thin voice, but to delight in song;
until age and ignorance rip through wrong:
Like a foolish child scolded by rain;
rightly thrust into the bed of swelling pain.

Broken by the rocks, left with only words;
plucking away at bloated fears like chords.
Now swelling up inside, breaking out unto,
the sea foam that forms puddles around you.

SILENT SEPTEMBER

Damp, crimson days when I succumb to envy:
Over visions of our Father in September; hence he,
upon sight of pink lace that adorns so gently,
sheath under-taking hands from gentry.
Touched ever tender, cause mind's tremor;
undone with worrisome, wrecked tenor.

By milky eye, extrinsic beasts break earthy tomb;
artifacts appropriated from would-be womb.
Divine form fracture, cross misty night;
ebony morn' — silent procession rap fright.
And though it shall be a repetitious clot,
desolate, mucky grave, obscure cellular rot.

INHARMONIOUS FINALE

Time is, but to pass light through recesses,
consuming bodies in youthful flutter.
The invisible tribe comes to dance and sing,
turning the wheel of truth over bodies;
smiles seemingly, breaking the shutter.

We cling tightly upon faded parchment;
written not with wicked tongue and strife,
but with a kaleidoscope of foreign words.
To pull us into a sea of serene emulation,
transforming shield and stone to knife.

Screaming out beyond the trees of nice,
breaking hand and feet, upon charlatan stone;
built with adorned, masquerading crimes.

For in the hour of waxy optics and blind sound,
admiration and facility will be seen as vice.
Swept away by rotting silhouettes;
clinging upon sustenance of finely laid chalk.

'Tis but nature's way to unravel precious thread,
and from the clumps of undigested dread,
spring forth newly established bedrocks.

In one's unfettered mind holds answer to reason;
though in time, mobs of virtue abuse treason.

In the ending hour, memories fizzle,
passing away into chunks of unrest.
They shake, flatten and wriggle,
breaching stone walls of solitude;
'til end draws nigh, of unresolved digest.

SYMPATHY FOR THE MASTIM

Doth he knoweth hate:
to hate and be hate;
to cleanse in suds of transient fear —
scatter like unsung note,
from mind's projected, frightful tear.

Doth he knoweth of the itch:
convulsive, captivating twitch;
that burrows in thy mind —
engorged larva, shifting to find.

Doth he knoweth of hands:
broken weary, wanting strands.
Sinful cloth that rips from oneself;
smile that furrows across thineself.

Doth he knoweth,
where thoughts dare campaign for frills of passion
—

pups plucked from would-be heaven;
pushing down innocence for sake of others;
in the end, devoid of love.

Doth he knoweth fallible expansion:
from rosy, tender, loving lips,
where pale words expel like fashion,
where sensual hope caress from hips.
Youthful, yearning, learning eye,
thrust into segregated sea, like ships.

Between one thigh, birth other;
in the ending hour of erotic sensation,
where two bodies meld into another.
Where weak souls, split by sedation,
dare not feather.

Peeling back flesh, to become docile —
where sunken eyes scatter across skin,
where adolescent hubris goes out of style;
transfixes fertile douht — births hostile.

When mind dares break further;
teaming, expansion of universe
collide in one's tattered head.
For in the finality of thought,
we become nothing:

no virtue, nor wicked thought,
no actual sin, or paragon untaught.

SILENT DEPRIVATION

The shackles near, they hold me tight;
troubled coat of arms, ready to take flight.
Fluster, fiery and red with melted feet;
you must break us, to suck upon the teat.

And I see you there, flesh and frozen pain;
reeling at the world, full of shattered shame.
Until I touch the wound, restitched as before;
you pound against mind till properly sore.

Together our belief collects a dreamy state
until again we lose it all to this cruel fate.
And once becomes two, three, and more,
until it all becomes a wrenching chore.

Inspiration passes away, leaving only dark;
for it is we that have the unwavering mark.
Expansion of life ill-prepared and unfair,
though we take solace in the hell — we share.

It is this sadness that constructs our domain;
my garden springs forth from hopeful rain.
And you will tend to husbandry and me to Sun,
to lie open in delight for the forthcoming fun.

But in cruel exodus, all will float away once more,
leaving our seasonal domicile broken and poor.
I will blind myself with warmth to block the pain;
you, my most cherished, will have to do the same.

LOUPE

Unable to fathom fear,
that furrow and seed.
I find myself breakin' glass,
to watch it bleed.

Through oculus affair,
crafted with childlike pane.
From clusters of sand,
an umbra of state restrain.

DREAM STATION

Day forever tosses and turns into night,
crafting unreasonable fright.
Pleasurable, waxy ascent;
causes refractions of mutual content.

Outreached fingers primed for accuracy:
moist touch, commercial pleasure — urgency.

Looking for truer sense of utterance;
the mind must impose artificial sustenance.
Ignorance's resound assimilation of freedom
with lent passage back to Eden.

Follow through, with identity absolved:
Sprawled legs, clenched hands — resolved.
Lost encounters, in search of the rest;
subscribes me to subconscious fears of jest.

Shelter from verities that gently touch me;
entranced by illusions, that could be.
A brown and rusted cage bequeathed;
capture ideals that have long been sheathed.

Watchful, panicked eyelid — cyclical delirium;
mind plastered, with sorely bruised ilium.
Wrapping preoccupied body, in warm delight,
till I reach the zenith of all mind's insight.

Tangled trail toward carnal consumption;
late to stimulate educated assumption.
'Tis not our right, not on splendid night,
to cut chord of this fantastical flight.

LOST IN ANNA

Fractured, unsavory glass in the sink;
mangled hands to make you think.
Meticulously monitoring as you woke;
you howled out fierce, and I spoke.
But you exploited me against better judgement;
an absorbent for feverish pain — abundant.

Collecting sorrow and shame for refinement;
to seek peace causes unneeded excitement.
So I stayed in this vacuous chamber for you;
to grasp something from the person inside true:
A fractal tarrying in darkness — breakthrough.

For him, you built makeshift cathedrals of agony,
reeling inside from past's immortal pain.
Slicing deep into mind's complex anatomy,
'til nothing remains but the residue of shame.

And I nothing more than bloodied, used linen,
would wrap barren soul in splendid virtue.
Sewing mouth and eye to bolster your condition,
in the end, lie unraveled in search of anew.

ANA IN STASIS

In darling, deepened dreams of my tears,
where child-like heart calls for you.
The shell never splattered cross,
a trembling-drenched face of fears.

Where body nevermore sank deep,
into sentiment, scarlet frock; for I keep,
though I watch it slowly turn black,
adorning upon grief-stricken back.

INDIFFERENT THOUGHTS

Why must the vulture bark his happy song;
does it not know of my unending wrong.
To call upon blurred memories breaks me;
tossing my frailty into a dizzying sea.

Take careful note to the recesses of my attempt:
Clouded lust, encapsulated reason, robust intent.
Prospect reflections of dreamy campaigns confined;
drink resin of organic ideals lost — battered and
primed.

ABOUT THE AUTHOR

Adeleine Keane is a poet and writer, blending contemporary elements with traditional ones. Keane's poetry most often touches on satirical subject matters, drawing awareness to the imprudence and nature of man.

Inspired by gothic, dark-wave, and folk musical elements, as well as epic storytelling and playful rhyming scheme, Adeleine Keane shifts from the darkness and utter destruction of man to the personal dilemma of losing one's loved one and unto more spry metrical stanzas about the fallacy of virtue and immorality.

For more books and updates:
www.adeleinekeane.com

www.ingramcontent.com/pod-product-compliance
Lightning Source LLC
Chambersburg PA
CBHW060509300726
48975CB00008B/2711